VARDIELLO

SILLY FELLOW

and other interesting folk

Compiled by Pat Edwards and Wendy Body

Acknowledgements

Ward Lock Educational Co. Ltd for the story 'Vardiello' from *Short Tales 1* by Geoffrey Summerfield (pub Ward Lock Educational Co. Ltd, 1980); Penguin Books Australia Ltd for the poem 'Brenda Baker' from *In The Garden of Badthings* by Doug MacLeod (pub Penguin Books Australia Ltd); Penguin Books Ltd for the poem 'I do not wish to harp about Lew' from p.46 *Songs For My Dog and Other People* by Max Fatchen (Kestrel Books, 1980) Copyright © 1980 by Max Fatchen; the author's agents for the story 'Lester and the Underground Treasure' from *The Adventures of Lester* By Quentin Blake; Oxford University Press for an extract from the short story 'Pippi Goes to the Circus' pp.99–116 *Pippi Longstocking* by Astrid Lingren trans. Edna Hurup (1954). Text and photographs for pages 50–53 were provided by David Jamieson.

Illustrators, other than those acknowledged with each story, include; Quentin Blake pp.18–32; Peter Dennis pp.52–53; Marjory Gardner pp.60–61; Gaspp pp.54–59; Bettina Gutheridge p.33; Rolf Heimann pp.34–35; Geoff Hocking pp.4–15; Cindy Hunnam pp.62–63; Liz Roberts pp.36–49; Allan Stomann p.64; Katie Thomas pp.16-17.

Contents

VARDIELLO

An Italian folktale retold by Geoffrey Summerfield,
illustrated by Geoff Hocking.

There was once a very sensible woman who
lived with her only son. His name was
Vardiello, and he was a real fool.

One day, the mother had to run an errand, and so she said to her silly lad: "Now, listen, I've got to go out for an hour or two. The old hen in the shed is sitting on a dozen eggs, and they should be hatching out soon. So you just make sure she stays on the eggs and keeps them warm. If she wanders off to go scratching about in the yard, just look sharp and see that she gets back to the nest, double quick. Or we shall have no chickens. You understand?"

"Don't you worry about a thing. I'll take care of everything," said Vardiello.

"And one more thing. That new pot in the cupboard. If you so much as nibble what's in that pot, you'll be dead before you can say Jack Robinson. So leave well alone."

"Thanks for the warning. I'll go nowhere near it."

Now, as soon as his mother had gone, Vardiello went into the garden, and he dug holes all over, and covered them with twigs and clods, to try to catch the lads that used to come scrumping in the apple-trees. He worked hard for an hour or more, and he was just rubbing his aching back when he saw the old hen come waddling into the garden for a good scratch-around.

"**B**ack you go! Shoo! Shoo! Hish! Hish! Back to your eggs! Go on!"

But the hen just ignored him. So he stamped his feet. Then he threw his cap at her. But it made no difference. The old hen just went on with her scratching. So Vardiello got into a real panic, and he picked up a big stick and threw it at her!

Bonk! It hit the poor old hen right on the head, and there she lay, in the dust, dead as a doornail.

"Oh, the eggs! The chickens!" Vardiello cried. And he rushed into the shed. He put his hand on the eggs and they were almost stone-cold. So he sat on them, to warm them up again, and his trousers were plastered with smashed eggs. What a mess! He tried to scrape it all off, but his hands were just smeared with goo, so he wriggled out of his trousers and washed them in the kitchen sink. He didn't have time to dry them, and they were his only pair, so he put them on again while they were still sopping wet, and his legs felt clammy from top to bottom.

By this time, he was so hungry that his stomach was rumbling like thunder. So he went out and found the poor old hen. He plucked her and cleaned her, lit a fire in the grate, and cooked her.

When the old hen was well cooked, he put her just outside the kitchen-door to cool off. Then he decided to do himself proud, and spread a clean cloth on the table. Then he went down to the cellar with a large jug to get some wine to drink with his meal: in those days, people didn't drink tea, but used to keep a great barrel of wine in the cellar, to drink with their meals.

So he put his jug under the tap of the barrel, and turned the tap on.

He was watching all the bubbles sparkling in the jug, when he heard a terrible clattering and banging upstairs. So he rushed out of the cellar, and there were two great tom-cats fighting over his chicken!

He chased those cats all over the yard, and they dashed into the house to hide. So he chased them all over the house, upstairs and downstairs, until the cats dropped the old hen under the bed. By the time he'd picked it up and cleaned it, he suddenly remembered the wine-tap: it was still running!

So he dashed down to the cellar, and the barrel was empty. The wine was all over the floor, a great flood.

Now he had to work out a plan to prevent his mother from finding out. He took a sack of flour, and scattered it all over the cellar floor, to soak up all the wine.

Then he sat down, and thought, "No fat hen! No eggs! No chickens! No wine! No flour! No hope!"

12

He didn't dare face his mother when she came back, so he decided to do away with himself. He remembered what she had said about the new pot in the cupboard. She'd said he would die if he even nibbled whatever was in that pot. So he rushed up out of the cellar, slipping and sliding on the flour paste on the floor, and rushed to the cupboard. He snatched the pot off the shelf and gulped down everything, glug, glug, munch, munch, until the pot was empty.

Then he went and hid in the oven, and waited to die.

W hen his mother got back, she knocked and knocked. She had always told him to lock the door when she went out, so she waited for him to come and open it. She knocked and knocked, then she knocked again until her knuckles were sore. Then she lost her patience and kicked the door open.

"Vardiello! Vardiello! Where are you? What are you up to? Are you deaf? Come out, come out, wherever you are! Do you hear?"

And a thin squeaky voice came out of the oven:

"I'm in here. In the oven. But you'll never see me again. I shall be dead in a minute!"

D on't talk daft!"

"But I shall. I've eaten the poison in the pot. And I'm dying."

Then his mother sat down and laughed until she cried. The tears poured down her face, and her handkerchief was soaking wet.

"Tell me all about it," she said, when she could speak. "You silly billy! Tell me what happened."

So he told her all about the old hen, the eggs, the cats, the wine, the flour, and the poison in the pot.

"Oh, the pot!" his mother said. "It was full of pickled walnuts. I was saving them for a rainy day. I just didn't want you to eat them. So I warned you to leave well alone! But they weren't poison. You'll just have a stomach ache. Now, come out of that oven and stretch your legs."

So Vardiello clambered out of the oven. And he felt very foolish.

Then his mother gave him a glass of milk.

(And Vardiello lived foolishly ever after.)

Meet two more Foolish Folk

Brenda Baker

Brenda Baker, quite ill-bred,
Used to cuddle fish in bed.
Tuna, trout and conger-eels,
Salmon, sole and sometimes seals.
Barracuda, bream and bass,
She cuddled them, until – alas!
One unforgotten Friday night
She slept with two piranhas,
And, being rather impolite,
They ate her best pyjamas!

Doug MacLeod

Lew

I don't wish to harp about Lew
Who kept peering into the stew.
He lifted the lid
And in it he slid.
I think I'll miss dinner, don't you?

Max Fatchen

Lester and the Underground Treasure

Lester and Lorna and Otto were sitting under the Nothing tree.

Now you probably know that where Lester lives, nearly everything you need grows on trees. There's a clothes tree; a tree for boots-and-shoes; a tree for buns-and-cakes, and a tree that grows frying pans and dustbins and all kinds of things like that — it's called the General Hardware tree.

But there was one tree that was not at all like the others. It was called the Nothing tree, and there was nothing on it. No shoes, no cakes, no dustbins — nothing. Just a few little whiskers. Nobody knew why. It was a mystery.

"The Nothing tree is all right," said Lorna, "but there isn't very much that you can *do* with it. I think it's time for something exciting to happen."

Lorna was always wanting something exciting to happen. Sometimes it didn't; sometimes it did. Anyway, just then along came Old Junk with his sack. Lorna asked him if he had anything exciting in his sack. Old Junk put his sack down on the ground and said: "Well, we'll have a little look and see what there is. Now then — " and he rummaged about in the sack. The first thing he pulled out was a set of false teeth for a small dinosaur.

"How about that?" he said. "Nice sharp little set".

Lorna said they were quite exciting but not exciting enough, and had he got anything else.

The next thing was: some trousers for a three-legged dwarf. "You don't often see a pink and blue tartan," said Old Junk, but Lorna decided they were not very exciting.

Lester and Otto kept looking eagerly in case the next thing was something really good, because you never knew what Old Junk might have in his sack. The next thing he pulled out was: a plastic bucket of cold porridge.

"Only slightly dusty," said Old Junk, flicking it with the dwarf's trousers; but Lorna said that it was not exciting *at all*. And it began to look as though there was nothing interesting in the sack, when Old Junk dipped in again and brought out a little rolled-up piece of paper. He gave it to Lester, and Lester unrolled it. It seemed to be some kind of plan or map. Lorna and Otto looked over his shoulder, and this is what they could see:

"Treasure," said Lorna. "Now that *is* exciting."
Otto wasn't quite so sure. "Er — how are we
going to see in the dark tunnel?" he said. "I
suppose you wouldn't have a torch in the sack as
well?" asked Lester.

Old Junk groped about in the sack. He hadn't
got a torch, but he found an old luminous nose.
Lorna put it on with elastic that went round the
back of her head. She thought that looking for
treasure was going to be smashing.

And so they thanked Old Junk for his presents,
and with Flap-eared Lorna proudly wearing her
luminous nose and rollerskating ahead, they set
off on their treasure-hunt.

Otto still wasn't sure that looking for treasure was a good idea, and he kept saying things like, "But where *is* this Look-out tree?" and "How shall we *know* it's the Look-out tree?" Lester explained that they would know it when they saw it because it was the kind of tree you could climb up into and then look out for treasure.

"There's one," he said.

It was a short tree with a fluffy top. They went
to have a look at it; but when they got near they
discovered it was only Fuzzy William. He is
someone who looks rather like a giant at the top
and rather like a dwarf at the bottom.

So they went on until they came to a little hill,
with two trees on it, and they thought it might be
one of them. But when they got round the other
side they discovered it was a tall bird. It was lying
on the ground with its legs in the air, having a
little sleep.

"Better not wake it up," said Lorna. "It looks tired."

Then they saw something rather strange. Could it be a Look-out tree? It had a lot of things waving about in the air that might be branches. But when they got a bit closer they found it was Plunkett-Vere-Smith. He was waving all his three heads and five legs and seven arms because he was having an argument with a snake about whether it was a good thing to have legs or not.

25

The trouble with Plunkett-Vere-Smith is that he is really like three people, and he can never agree with himself about anything. Lester knew it was no good asking him where the Look-out tree was, because he would only point in seven different directions at once. So they asked the snake, and he said: "Just keep straight on, you can't miss it."

The tree they came to didn't look anything very special. In fact it was just an ordinary General Hardware tree, with its branches sprouting all the usual things like dustbins and buckets and vegetable strainers.

They were standing underneath it wondering who was to climb up and look out for the treasure, when there was a clattering noise among the branches. Flap-eared Lorna shouted:

"LOOK OUT!"

and a heavy flat-iron came whizzing down out of the tree and landed with a thump on the ground. Now they knew why it was called the Look-out tree.

Lester and Otto had jumped out of the way. Otto was rolling about on the ground, and trembling with shock. Lorna got hold of him and stood him the right way up. "Oh Lorna," he said, wiping his brow, "I knew this treasure-hunting wasn't a good idea!"

They looked round for Lester. He seemed to have disappeared completely. But then they saw a big hole in the ground, and they heard Lester's voice say: "I'm down here. It's very dark."

"This way," said Lorna and she started off down the hole. Otto went after her. Once they got into the darkness Lorna's luminous nose gave a lovely glow. They could easily see Lester, and a narrow tunnel sloping away under the ground. They set off to look for the treasure.

They seemed to walk for quite a long time, and there was no sign of any treasure. No sign of anything in fact. Otto wasn't at all happy. He had been nearly hit by a flat-iron and now here he was lost in the dark.

But then suddenly there was more light. A trap-door opened in front of them, and a face looked out. It was one of the gnomes that live underground. They have lamps in their hats so that they can see where they are going, and it was one of these lamps that was giving the extra light.

"Hello there, gorgeous," said the gnome.
"What a lovely luminous nose! You're a lucky girl.
I have an awful lot of trouble with the lamp in my
hat." He was quite right — you could see the
beam of the lamp bending round the wrong way,
and in fact pointing every way except the right
one. Lorna said that if he showed them where the
treasure was he could have the luminous nose.

"You're on," he said, and he climbed out of his
hole, closed the trap-door, and began to lead them
along the underground tunnel. They could tell
they were going up and down, and round bends,
and they could see the sides of the tunnel, which
were made of earth, shining in the light of the
luminous nose and the gnome's lamp as it twisted
this way and that.

They seemed to have gone quite a long way
when the gnome stopped and said: "There it is."
And there it was: lots and lots of toffees and
chocolates in shiny wrappings, hundreds of them
in great clusters and bunches, sprouting out of
tangled roots coming through the earth.

Lester said: "The treasure."
Lorna said: "*Whooppee.*"
Otto thought: "I'm quite glad I came."

They picked off an armful of sweets and chocolates each, and were thinking that they would have to set out to walk all the way back, when some earth started to fall down from the roof of the tunnel, and a face appeared. It was the face of the tall bird, and his head came down through a hole that he had made in the ground.

"Hello," he said. "Just looking about for worms and seeds and things."

And so, to save going all the way back, they handed over the luminous nose to the underground gnome, who said, "It fits a treat" as he fastened the elastic round his head. Then they climbed through the hole up the tall bird's neck. When they clambered out and looked round they were very surprised indeed: because there in front of them, where they'd been sitting not so long ago was the Nothing tree.

"So *that's* why there's nothing," said Lorna. "All the time there were all those lovely toffees and chocolates," said Otto, "under the ground." "And we never knew," said Lester. And then they took an armful of sweets each and climbed up into the branches of the Nothing tree. When they got there, they gave some to the tall bird and told him all about their exciting search for the underground treasure.

Written and illustrated by *Quentin Blake*

The well-prepared treasure-seeker

torch for searching in dark caves...

cap with brim (to keep sun out of eyes)

super-light backpack to hold treasure. It also has water bottle, lunch box, first aid kits, spare torch batteries, matches.

compass

chewing gum and barley sugar

walkie-talkie

watch

treasure-map, pen and paper

climbing-rope

loose-fitting comfortable trousers

pocket for nuts and fruit to nibble

thick, wool socks, so you won't get blisters

heavy walking boots

shovel to dig for treasure

Treasure Island

Jellyfish Beach

Haunted Mountain

Lonely Clif[f]

Lake Loon

Golden River

Ice-Cream Mountains

Walk warily—Monsters live here.

Good spot for panning gold

The Ghostly Forest (Beware of ferocious lions)

Smoky Woods

Golden River

Phantom Creek

Giant Marigolds grow here

Marshmallow Lake

Good camping spot

Sweetwater River

Whispering Waterfall

Home of the Talk[ing] Rhuba[rb] (Keep away)

Pirate Cove (Safe for all pirate ships)

Black Rocks

Shark Beach

Captain's Headland

A fun map

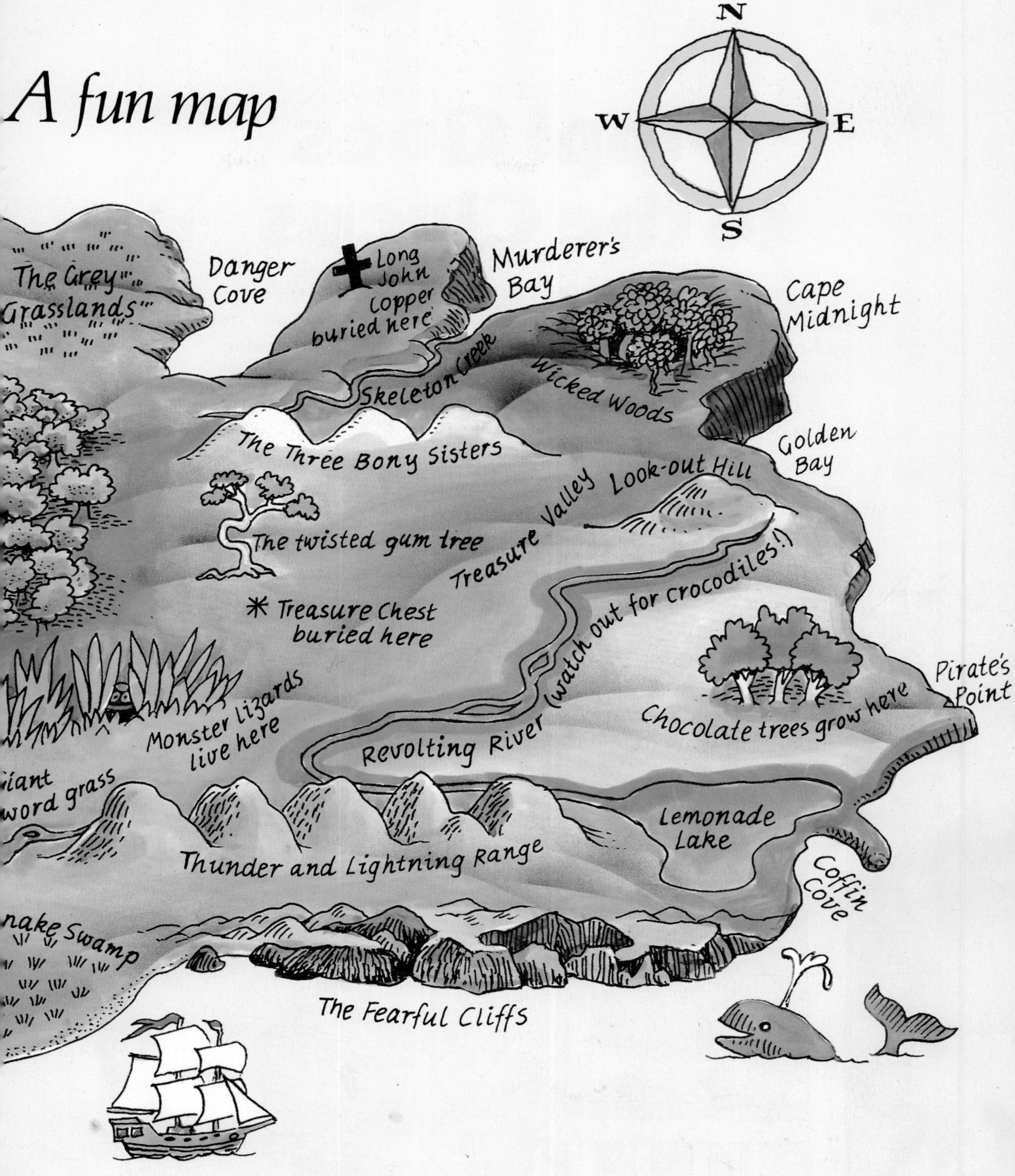

N
W   E
S

The Grey Grasslands

Danger Cove

Long John Copper buried here

Murderer's Bay

Cape Midnight

Skeleton Creek

Wicked Woods

The Three Bony Sisters

Golden Bay

The twisted gum tree

Treasure Valley

Look-out Hill

* Treasure Chest buried here

Monster lizards live here

Revolting River (watch out for crocodiles!)

Chocolate trees grow here

Pirate's Point

Giant sword grass

Thunder and Lightning Range

Lemonade Lake

Coffin Cove

Snake Swamp

The Fearful Cliffs

Pippi Goes to the Circus

Pippi Longstocking is the only girl in the world who can do exactly what she likes! She is nine years old, very strong and lives by herself in a cottage in Sweden. She has a horse and a monkey for company. She also has two friends called Tommy and Annika.

A circus had come to the little town, and all the children ran to their mothers and fathers and begged to be allowed to go. Tommy and Annika did so too, and their kind father at once gave them some of the shiny Swedish silver coins called crowns.

With their money held tightly in their hands, they rushed over to Pippi. She was on the front porch with the horse, arranging his tail into small braids, each tied with a red ribbon.

"Today is his birthday, I think," she said, "so he has to be dressed up."

"Pippi," said Tommy, panting, for they had run so fast, "Pippi, can you come with us to the circus?"

"I can do anything I please," said Pippi, "but I don't know if I can come to the sarcus, 'cause I don't know what a sarcus is. Does it hurt?"

"How silly you are!" said Tommy. "It doesn't hurt! It's just fun! Horses and clowns and beautiful ladies who walk on a rope!"

"But it costs money," said Annika, opening her little hand to see if her three shiny crowns still lay there.

"I'm rich as a goblin," said Pippi, "so I suppose I can always buy a sarcus. It's going to be crowded if I have any more horses, though. The clowns and those beautiful ladies could squeeze into the laundry-house, but it's more of a problem with the horses."

"What nonsense!" said Tommy. "You're not going to *buy* the circus. It costs money to go there and look, don't you see?"

"Heaven help me!" cried Pippi, shutting her eyes tight. "Does it cost money to *look*? And here I've been going around with my eyes open all day and every day! Goodness knows how much money I've used up already!"

Then little by little she carefully opened one eye, and rolled it round and round in her head. "Cost what it will" she said, "I must have a peep now!"

Tommy and Annika finally succeeded in explaining to Pippi what a circus was, and then Pippi went and took some gold pieces out of her suitcase. After that she put on her hat, which was as big as a mill-wheel, and they started off for the circus.

There was a crowd of people outside the circus tent, and in front of the ticket window stood a long queue. By and by it was Pippi's turn. She stuck her head through the window, looked hard at the dear old lady who sat there, and said, "How much does it cost to look at *you*?"

The old lady was from a foreign country, so she didn't understand what Pippi meant. She answered, "Liddle girl, it is costink vive crones the front rows and dree crones the back rows and wan crones the zdandinkroom."

"I see," said Pippi. "But you must promise that you'll walk on the rope too."

Now Tommy stepped in and said that Pippi would have a ticket for the back rows. Pippi gave a gold piece to the old lady, and she looked suspiciously at it. She bit it, too, to see if it were real. At last she was convinced that it really was gold, and Pippi got her ticket. She got a great many silver coins in change as well.

"What do I want with all that nasty little white money?" said Pippi crossly. "Keep it. I'll look at you twice instead. From the zdandinkroom."

So, as Pippi absolutely didn't want any money back, the lady changed her ticket for a front row one, and gave Tommy and Annika front row tickets as well, without their having to add any money of their own. In this way, Pippi and Tommy and Annika came to sit on some very fine red chairs by the ringside. Tommy and Annika turned round several times in order to wave to their schoolmates, who sat much farther away.

"*This* is a queer hut," said Pippi, looking about her with wonder. "But they've spilled sawdust on the floor, I see. Not that I'm fussy, but it *does* look a bit untidy."

Tommy explained to Pippi that there was always sawdust in circus rings for the horses to run on.

On a platform sat the circus musicians, and they suddenly began to play a rousing march. Pippi clapped her hands wildly and jumped up and down in her chair with delight.

"Does it cost something to listen, too, or can you do that free?" she wondered.

Just then the curtain was pulled back from the artistes' entrance, and the ringmaster, dressed in black and with a whip in his hand, came running in, and with him there came ten white horses with red plumes on their heads.

40

The ringmaster cracked his whip, and the horses cantered round the ring. Then he cracked his whip again, and they all stood with their front legs up on the railing which circled the ring. One of the horses had stopped just in front of the children. Annika didn't like having a horse so close to her, so she crouched back in her chair as far as she could. But Pippi leaned forward, lifted up the horse's front leg, and said, "How's yourself? My horse sends his regards to you. It's *his* birthday too today, though he has bows on his tail instead of his head."

As luck would have it, Pippi let go of the horse's foot before the ringmaster cracked his whip the next time, because then all the horses jumped down from the railing and began to canter again.

When the act was finished, the ringmaster bowed beautifully, and the horses trotted out. A second later the curtain opened again for a coal-black horse, and on his back stood a beautiful lady dressed in green silk tights. Her name was Miss Carmencita, it said in the programme.

The horse trotted round in the sawdust, and Miss Carmencita stood there calmly and smiled. But then something happened. Just as the horse passed Pippi's place, something came whistling through the air. It was none other than Pippi herself. There she suddenly stood on the horse's back behind Miss Carmencita. At first, Miss Carmencita was so astonished that she nearly fell off the horse. Then she became angry. She began to hit behind herself with her hands in order to get Pippi to jump off. But she couldn't manage it.

"Calm down a little," said Pippi. "You're not the only one who's going to have fun. There are others who've paid *their* money too, believe it or not!"

Then Miss Carmencita wanted to jump off herself, but she couldn't do that either, for Pippi had a steady hold round her waist. The people in the circus couldn't help laughing. It looked so silly, they thought, to see the beautiful Miss Carmencita held fast by a little red-headed scamp who stood on the horse's back in her big shoes looking as if she'd never done anything *but* perform in a circus.

But the ringmaster didn't laugh. He made a sign to his red-coated attendants to run forward and stop the horse.

"Is the act over already?" said Pippi, disappointed. "Just now when we were having such fun !"

"Derrible child," hissed the ringmaster between his teeth, "go avay!"

Pippi looked sorrowfully at him. "Well, but, now," she said, "why are you so angry with me? I thought everyone was supposed to have a nice time here."

She jumped down from the horse, and went and sat down in her place. But now two big attendants came to throw her out. They took hold of her and tried to lift her.

It was no use. Pippi just sat still, and it simply wasn't possible to move her from the spot, though they tugged as hard as they could. So they shrugged their shoulders and went away.

In the meantime the next act had begun. It was Miss Elvira, who was to walk the tight-rope. She wore a pink tulle dress and caried a pink parasol in her hand. With small neat steps she ran out on to the rope. She swung her legs and did all manner of tricks. It was very pretty indeed. She proved too that she could go backwards on the thin rope. But when she came back to the little platform at the end of the line and turned round, Pippi was standing there.

"What was it you said?" said Pippi, delighted to see Miss Elvira's surprised expression.

Miss Elvira didn't say anything at all, but jumped down from the rope and threw her arms around the neck of the ringmaster, who was her father. Again he sent for his attendants to throw Pippi out. This time he sent for five. But all the people in the circus shouted, "Let her be! We want to see the little red-head!"

They all stamped their feet and clapped their hands.

Pippi ran out on the line. And Miss Elvira's tricks were nothing compared to what Pippi could do. When she came to the middle of the rope, she stretched one leg straight up into the air, and her big shoe spread out like a roof over her head. She waggled her foot a little, to scratch behind her ear.

The ringmaster was not the least bit pleased that Pippi was performing in his circus. He wanted to be rid of her. So he sneaked forward and loosened the mechanism which held the line tight, and he was sure that Pippi would fall off.

But she didn't. She began to swing the rope instead. Back and forth swayed the line, faster and faster swung Pippi, and then – suddenly – she took a leap into the air and landed right on the ringmaster. He was so frightened that he began to run.

"This horse is even more fun," said Pippi. "But why haven't you any tassels in your hair?"

Now Pippi thought it was time to turn back to Tommy and Annika. She climbed off the ringmaster and went and sat down, and then the next act was about to begin. There was a moment's delay, because the ringmaster first had to go out and drink a glass of water and comb his hair. But after that he came in, bowed to the audience, and said, "Ladies and chantlemen! In ze next moment you vill zee vun of ze vunders uff all time, ze zdrongest man in ze vorld, Mighty Adolf, who nobody has effer beaten yet. And here he is, ladies and chantlemen. Mighty Adolf!"

A gigantic man stepped into the ring. He was dressed in scarlet tights, and he had a leopard skin round his stomach. He bowed to the audience, and looked very self-satisfied indeed.

"Just *look* at which mossels!" said the ringmaster, squeezing Mighty Adolf's arm where the muscles bulged like bowls under the skin.

"And now, ladies and chantlemen, I giff you a grrreat offer! Weech of you dares to try a wrestling match with Mighty Adolf, who dares to try to beat ze world's zdrongest man? A hundred crowns I pay to the vun who can beat Mighty Adolf. A hundred crowns, consider it, ladies and chantlemen! Step right up! Who'll giff it a try?"

Nobody came forward.

"What did he say?" asked Pippi. "And why is he speaking Arabian?"

"He said that the person who can beat that great big man over there will get a hundred crowns," said Tommy.

"I can do it," said Pippi. "But I think it would be a shame to beat him, 'cause he looks such a nice man."

"But you could *never* do it," said Annika. "Why, that's the strongest man in the world!"

"Man, yes," said Pippi. "But I'm the strongest *girl* in the world, don't forget."

In the meanwhile, Mighty Adolf was lifting dumb-bells and bending thick iron bars to show how strong he was.

"Now, now, goot people!" shouted the ringmaster. "Is there rilly nobody who should like to vin a hundred crowns? Must I rilly keep them for myself?" he said, waving a hundred-crown note.

"No, I rilly don't think you must," said Pippi, climbing over the railing to the ring.

"Go! Disappear! I don't vant I should zee you," the ringmaster hissed.

"Why are you always so unfriendly?" said Pippi reproachfully. "I only want to fight with Mighty Adolf."

"Zis is no time for chokes," said the ringmaster. "Go avay, before Mighty Adolf hears your impertinence!"

But Pippi went right past the ringmaster and over to Mighty Adolf. She took his big hand in hers and shook it heartily.

"Now, shall we have a bit of a wrestle, you and I?" she said.

Mighty Adolf looked at her and didn't understand a thing.

"In one minute I'm going to begin," said Pippi.

And she did. She grappled properly with Mighty Adolf, and before anyone knew how it had happened, she'd laid him flat on the mat. Mighty Adolf scrambled up, quite red in the face.

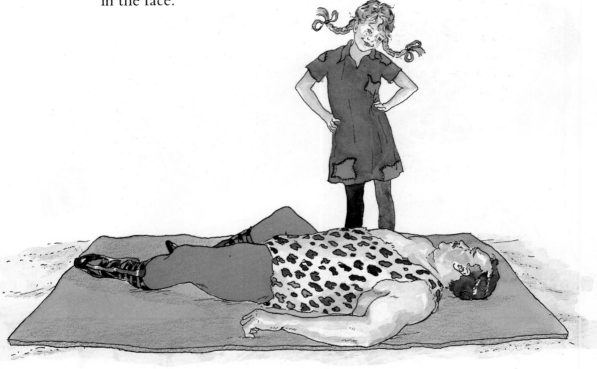

"Hurrah for Pippi!" shouted Tommy and Annika. All the people at the circus heard this, and so they shouted, "Hurrah for Pippi!" too. The ringmaster sat on the railing and wrung his hands. He was angry. But Mighty Adolf was angrier still. Never in his life had anything so terrible happened to him. But now he would show this little red-haired girl what kind of a man Mighty Adolf was! He rushed forward and took a strong grip on her, but Pippi stood as fast as a rock.

"You can do better than that," she said to encourage him. Then she pried herself free from his grip, and in a second, Mighty Adolf was lying on the mat again. Pippi stood beside him and waited. She didn't have to wait long. With a bellow he raised himself and stormed at her again.

"Tiddlelipom and poddeliday," said Pippi.

All the people at the circus stamped their feet and threw their caps up in the air, and shouted, "Hurrah for Pippi!"

The third time Mighty Adolf rushed at her, Pippi lifted him high into the air and carried him on her upstretched arms around the ring. After that, she laid him on the mat and held him there.

48

"Now, my boy, I think we've had enough of this sort of game," she said. "It won't get any more fun than this, anyway."

"Pippi is the winner! Pippi is the winner!" shouted all the people at the circus. Mighty Adolf slunk out as fast as he could. And the ringmaster had to go forward and present Pippi the hundred-crown note, though he looked as if he would rather have eaten her up.

"Here you are, my young lady, here is your hundred crowns!"

"That?" said Pippi scornfully. "What should I do with that piece of paper? You can have it to wrap fish in, if you want!"

Then she went back to her place.

"This is a long-lasting circus, this one," she said to Tommy and Annika. "Forty winks might not do any harm. But wake me if there's anything else I need to help with."

So she lay back in her chair and went to sleep immediately. There she lay snoring while clowns and sword-swallowers and snake-people showed their tricks to Tommy and Annika and all the other people at the circus.

"Somehow, I think Pippi was best of all," whispered Tommy to Annika.

Written by Astrid Lindgren,
illustrated by Liz Roberts

CIRCUS SCRAPBOOK

Did you know that the circus began in London? In 1768, Philip Astley roped off a ring to give trick riding shows.

Soon there were acts by clowns, tightrope walkers and acrobats too . . . and the circus was born!

The ringmaster runs the circus show. He welcomes you and tells you about the acts you see. He makes sure all the props and rigging are there for each act. David Hibling at the Great Yarmouth Circus has to speak several languages, as the artistes come from all over the world.

Yasmine Smart fell in love with horses when she was very young. Now she has her own Arabian horses. She was the first British artiste to win a Silver Clown award at the Monte Carlo Circus Festival.

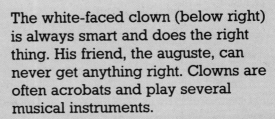

The white-faced clown (below right) is always smart and does the right thing. His friend, the auguste, can never get anything right. Clowns are often acrobats and play several musical instruments.

These acrobats are from Morocco in North Africa. They have to be strong and they have to work as a team, otherwise this human pyramid would fall down.

Animals are an important part of the circus. They need to be properly looked after. David Taylor, the zoo vet, is giving this elephant from Austen Brothers' Circus her regular check-up.

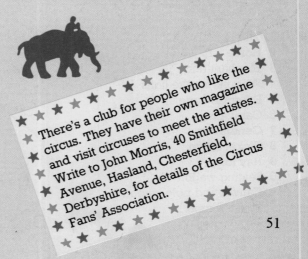

There's a club for people who like the circus. They have their own magazine and visit circuses to meet the artistes. Write to John Morris, 40 Smithfield Avenue, Hasland, Chesterfield, Derbyshire, for details of the Circus Fans' Association.

A travelling CIRCUS

The circus is like a small town of people and animals who live and work together. When the last show is over, everything is packed on to the trucks and moved to the next town. It takes about two hours for the seats and big top to be pulled down and about three hours for them to be built up the next day, ready for the first show.

The animals live near to the big top and all the artistes and workers have caravans. Generators make electricity for the lights and the heaters.

Key

1 The big top
2 Horse tent
3 Elephant tent
4 Wagons for the lions
5 Exercise cage
6 Caravans
7 Generators
8 Ticket office
9 Hay lorry
10 Seating wagon
11 Canvas and pole wagon
12 Toilet wagon

Before the circus arrives in a town, colourful posters and adverts in newspapers tell you that it's coming.

53

In the year AD 64, the Roman Emperor Nero's best-kept secret was his recipe for a delicious dessert made from snow and fruit juices.

Would you like my recipe for Chinese frozen milk?...

Hundreds of years later Italian explorer, Marco Polo, returned from his long trip to China with a recipe for a kind of ice-cream made from milk.

Yum, Yum!

Let's have it every night!

It wasn't long before all the Kings and Queens of Europe were tucking in to ice-cream. England's King Charles I (who died in 1649) loved it so much he bribed a French ice-cream maker to produce special ice-cream just for him. Like Nero, he tried to make sure the recipe was kept secret, but somehow it leaked out (or should we say dripped?).

O n 17th May, 1784 George Washington, first American President, made an important decision. He bought an ice-cream machine!

T here were no fridges in those days, so it was just as well he didn't have to make his own. It took hours and hours of shaking before the mixture of milk or cream, eggs and flavouring hardened.

Ordinary people didn't have it often.

Then in 1848 along came a brainy lady named Nancy Johnson.

She put a crank on her bucket and hey presto — a new ice-cream machine!

Now that it was much easier to make ice-cream it didn't take long before street sellers were offering the delicious treat to anyone who was strolling around the parks or towns.

57

I
ce-cream sodas were created quite by accident in 1850

and the first ice-cream factory was built in 1851.

S
unday became the popular day to go out and buy ice-cream, so some bright seller invented the ice-cream sundae (carefully changing the name a little so the churches would not be upset).

Until 1904 ice-cream was always sold in a dish and you needed a spoon to eat it with. And then the ice-cream cone was invented — again quite by accident.

Hmmm... I wonder if they'd go for this?

Charles Menches was selling ice-cream at an American fair when he ran out of dishes. A Syrian friend nearby was selling crisp, thin pastries called zalabia. Charles rolled up a zalabia, scooped ice-cream on top and hey presto again — the ice-cream cone was born!

Now, every year in every country millions of gallons of ice-cream are made and eaten.

And ice-cream lovers are living happily ever after.

61

Castor sugar is best.

You need: 2 eggs
½ cup of sugar
1 cup of cream
some crushed or sliced fruit

Or just sprinkle on some hundreds and thousands.

Separate the egg yolks from the whites

egg yolks   egg whites

Beat the egg whites with an egg-beater until they are white and stiff. Then add the sugar, a little at a time. When the mixture is shiny, add the egg yolks and beat and beat

and BEAT!

We're being beaten to death!

In another bowl, whip the cream until it is thick but not too stiff.

Very slowly stir the cream into the egg mixture. DON'T BEAT IT!

Pour into a refrigerator ice-cream tray and freeze until it sets.

Serve with fruit.

Genuine ice-cream-flavoured words

Glossary

argument (*p. 25*)
quarrel

braids (*p. 36*)
plaits

bribed (*p. 55*)
paid the ice-cream
maker money so
he would do
what he asked

brow (*p. 27*)
forehead

cantered (*p. 41*)
ran (horses)

clammy (*p. 8*)
sticky and damp

clods (*p. 6*)
lumps of earth

crank (*p. 57*)
a handle which makes
it easier to turn
something

do himself proud (*p. 10*)
treat himself very well

dozen (*p. 5*)
twelve

fits a treat (*p. 31*)
fits very well

flat-iron (*p. 26*)
an old-fashioned iron

grate (*p. 9*)
the part of a fireplace
where a fire is lit

harp (*p. 17*)
go on and on
about something

luminous (*p. 22*)
glowing or shining
with light

rummaged (*p. 20*)
searched

run an errand (*p. 5*)
to take a message or
fetch something

tartan (*p. 20*)
patterned woollen
material used to
make Scottish kilts